THE BEAR
DETECTIVES

**For Rory Anderson,
who listened to me telling stories
on October 13, 2008
S.G.**

**For Betty
J.B.**

ORCHARD BOOKS
338 Euston Road, London NW1 3BH
Orchard Books Australia
Hachette Children's Books
Level 17/207 Kent Street, Sydney NSW 2000

First published in the UK in 2009
First paperback publication in 2010

Text © Sally Grindley 2009
Illustrations © Jo Brown 2009

The rights of Sally Grindley to be identified as the author and
Jo Brown to be identified as the illustrator of this work
have been asserted by them in accordance with the
Copyright, Designs and Patents Act, 1988.

ISBN 978 1 84616 156 8 (hardback)
ISBN 978 1 84616 164 3 (paperback)

1 3 5 7 9 10 8 6 4 2 (hardback)
1 3 5 7 9 10 8 6 4 2 (paperback)

Printed in China

Orchard Books is a division of Hachette Children's Books,
an Hachette UK company.

www.hachette.co.uk

The Strange
Pawprint

Written by **SALLY GRINDLEY**
Illustrated by **JO BROWN**

ORCHARD BOOKS

Constable Tiggs

Sergeant Bumble

Albert

One cold, snowy morning, the
Bear Detectives were woken by
a loud knocking.
"Wake up! Wake up!" somebody
shouted.

Constable Tiggs leapt out of his bed and ran downstairs.

He found Albert, the repair-bear,
on the doorstep. "What on earth
has happened?" he said, shivering.

"I was checking the ground for holes, which is difficult in all this snow, when I found a strange pawprint," said Albert.

"What sort of strange?" asked Tiggs. "It looks as if the thing that made it has no fur, no pads and no hooves," said Albert. "And there are more strange pawprints in the park."

"I'd better fetch Sergeant Bumble," said Tiggs.

He bounded upstairs and knocked on his bedroom door. "Wake up, Sergeant Bumble!" he called.

The door opened and Bumble's
sleepy head appeared.
"What's all the noise?"
he asked grumpily.

"Albert's found a strange pawprint in the snow. The thing that made it has no fur and no pads and no hooves," said Tiggs.

"Then we must have a look at it,"
said Bumble. "Get dressed, Constable
Tiggs, quickly now!"

A few minutes later, the two
detectives followed Albert to
the first pawprint.

"You're right, Albert," Bumble nodded, studying it closely. "That is very strange."

"What do you think made it?"
asked Albert.

"Something very large," said
Bumble. "This is serious! We must
tell everyone to stay indoors until
we find out who, or what, made
this pawprint."

They set off through the snow,
knocking on doors and warning
the villagers to stay inside.

When at last they had spoken to all of them, they headed back to the police house to search through their Book of Unusual Pawprints.

"Now, let me see," said Bumble.

"Could it be a turtle?"

"No, Sir," said Tiggs. "Turtles have
flippers and pointy toes."

"A penguin, perhaps?" asked Bumble.

"Too small," said Tiggs.

"What about an elephant, then?"
asked Bumble.
"It could be an elephant!" cried
Tiggs excitedly. "They're very big
and they haven't got fur or pads
or hooves."

"We'll have to go outside and
see if we can spot the scoundrel,"
said Bumble.

It was snowing harder. Every little
sound made them jump.

"I'm s-scared," shivered Tiggs.

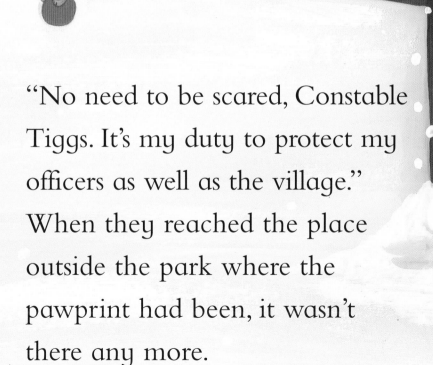

"No need to be scared, Constable Tiggs. It's my duty to protect my officers as well as the village." When they reached the place outside the park where the pawprint had been, it wasn't there any more.

"It's gone!" exclaimed Bumble.
"The snow must have filled it in,"
explained Tiggs.
"Of course," said Bumble quickly.
"That's just what I was going to say."

The other pawprints had gone as well. Tiggs began to shiver as they searched to see if any new ones had appeared.

"I think we'd better go back into the warm," said Bumble. "If that elephant has any sense it won't come out again today."

They hurried back to the police house, where they sat in front of the fire and warmed their feet.

"It is hard being a detective sometimes," mused Bumble. "While we face great danger, the other villagers can feel safe behind closed doors."

"Do you think we'll find some
more pawprints in the
morning?" asked Tiggs.
"I won't be surprised if
we do," said Bumble.

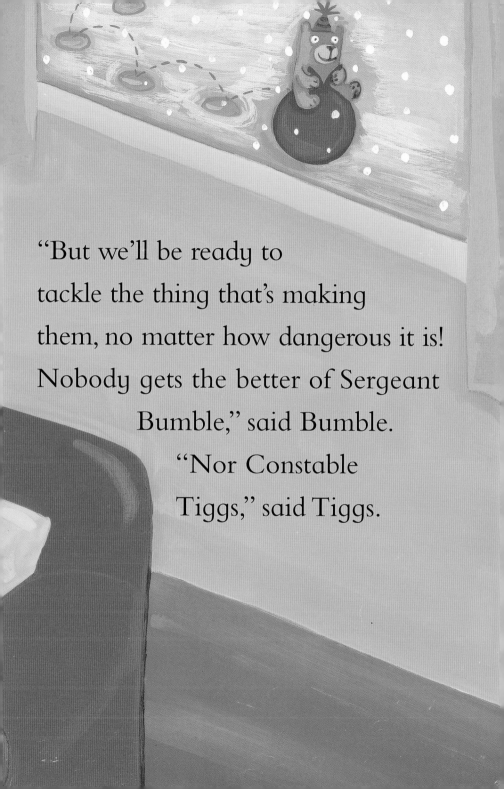

"But we'll be ready to
tackle the thing that's making
them, no matter how dangerous it is!
Nobody gets the better of Sergeant
Bumble," said Bumble.
"Nor Constable
Tiggs," said Tiggs.

THE BEAR DETECTIVES

SALLY GRINDLEY ❦ JO BROWN

Bucket Rescue	978 1 84616 152 0
Who Shouted Boo?	978 1 84616 109 4
The Ghost Train	978 1 84616 153 7
Treasure Hunt	978 1 84616 108 7
The Mysterious Earth	978 1 84616 155 1
The Strange Pawprint	978 1 84616 156 8
The Missing Spaghetti	978 1 84616 157 5
A Very Important Day	978 1 84616 154 4

All priced at £8.99

Orchard Colour Crunchies are available from all good bookshops,
or can be ordered direct from the publisher:
Orchard Books, PO BOX 29, Douglas IM99 1BQ
Credit card orders please telephone 01624 836000
or fax 01624 837033 or visit our website: www.orchardbooks.co.uk
or e-mail: bookshop@enterprise.net for details.

To order please quote title, author and ISBN
and your full name and address.
Cheques and postal orders should be made payable to 'Bookpost plc.'
Postage and packing is FREE within the UK
(overseas customers should add £2.00 per book).

Prices and availability are subject to change.